Poems to Sundry Notes of Jazz

JOHN TATUM

IN MEMORIAM
PETE BURDEN
The finest bebop alto anywhere

These poems were broadcast on BBC Radio Brighton in 1982 to the accompaniment of music by the PETE BURDEN quartet - Pete Burden, alto saxophone; Lionel Grigson, piano; Adrian Kendon, bass; Richard Johnson, drums; John Tatum, voice; and, on the last number, trumpet.

They were again broadcast in August of the same year, in a slightly enlarged version, on the BBC Radio 3 series, 'Jazz in Britain'. Original music was by Lionel Grigson and Adrian Kendon was musical director.

The Radio Brighton date was produced by Keith Slade and engineered by Piers Bishop. The Radio 3 date was presented by Charles Fox and produced by Pete Ritzema.

"The additional poems in this book have no special significance and are not connected in any way to the poems used in the radio broadcast.

My method of writing poetry is as follows: I keep a pad and a pen by the side of my bed and I wake up in the middle of the night with a few lines in my head (sometimes a whole poem) and just scribble them down. Then comes the real work; sometimes I work on a quite short poem for years until I get it right. The poems as they come to me could be about, for example, a gate leading into a muddy farmyard, an old car ... or someone playing the saxophone.

Through the years I wrote more poems in tune with my beloved musical genre and when I came to make this little book, it seemed like the right thing to do was to present them all together.

Some of the poems about jazz I sent to Pete White and Pete Burden because they seemed to enjoy them, which was a great honour to me."

CONTENTS

INTRODUCTION

Sunday morning.
Tube train
suddenly out
into flashing
sunlight.

Allotments,
fragments of field.

As weekly friends
filter into
the cold hall
a saxophone makes
exploring noises.

ELVIN JONES

Elephants. Big sides
swaying to and fro;
fragments of blazing
blue sky swaying
twixt drunken geographies
of tree-tops.
Parrots scrawl and rise,
flapping and screaming.

When will we get there?
Onwards, onwards,
slowly, slowly, like time.

The queen awaits us.
The witch doctor
throws the bones
on the fire.

PETE BURDEN

Twisting and turning,
thrusting through the soil;
slyly altering
the self-assured position
of rocks, creating countless
little caverns
for the lizard and the beetle
and the toad. On and on,
eternally, so no eye
could ever follow it,
no sharp pen repeat it;
twisting and turning
tangleroot life,
grubbing through the good earth,
echoing,
in countless skeins of light,
through the heavens ...

DON CHERRY

Hands slam into drums
and a bowl of burning incense
is offered
to the spirit of an ancestor
in an ancient tree.
If they did but know
the tree contains
more of that ancestor
than spirit. The very
molecules of its being
once formed part of him.
And, although he cannot speak
(save by the movement
of leaves in the wind)
he lives among them still.

DIZZY GILLESPIE

Down on a country-sized plain,
indistinct in sun-dazzle,
zebras mooch the trail of
Zulu armies. Suddenly, a speck of
yellow sparks and strikes.

Golden the sun and golden the lion
in prime of youth who
leaps and scatters fat grass-eaters,
live and frightened and running,
except for the one she's chosen.

So soon and sad the gold dims. The
pelt is worn bare and she snuffles for
insects, tail trailing away into
evening shadows and arthritic cold.

Published in OSTINATO

DIZZY BIG BAND

The mind, purged of worry
and distracting thought,
breaks free and is alive
to truth and pure sensation.

There is only root, bole and branch
and life returning to
and endlessly springing from
the Holy loam.

The drums pulse, the trumpet
soars and souls light up
with sudden smiles, beholding
the enigma of the universe.

WOODY HERMAN

Roots twisting and turning,
thrusting through the good earth;
clouds racing with the wind.

Sinuous saxophones,
searing trumpets,
inexorably moving.

Up front
an old man
jumps for joy.

JOHN COLTRANE

Drums thud,
feet stomp on the earth.
Tree-tops
reverberate and leaves
skitter in starlight.

An idol sits in his
hollow in a tree-trunk.
Glinting firelight,
flickering shadows of dancers
caress his wooden face.

He smiles
and they know their crops
have not been planted in vain.

THELONIOUS MONK

High over the town
he sits dreaming
on a park bench,
sounding his great
chords
over the sea.
The spinning sun
sinks forever in the
west
and a tired wind
shuffles round
his feet.

SONNY ROLLINS

His eyes, expressionless
like pebbles, cause us
to fidget in our seats.
His mind, behind them,
straddles the cosmos.
He pipes an endless
enigmatic note,
sucking in air
through the soles of his feet.
Suddenly,
in a flurry of twisted notes,
a nursery rhyme
lands, gurgling, in our laps.

Our dreams are blown to fragments
by the ventilator fan.

OH, DEAR!

Oh, dear! I'm broke again!
Spent all my bread
erecting a GIANT PHOTOGRAPH
of Sonny Rollins
at the end of the pier!
Everyone passing by says:
"Look. Who's that?"

Spoken in unison by Charles Fox,
Lionel Grigson, Pete Burden,
Adrian Kendon, Richard Johnson,
John Tatum, and divers engineers.

Published in OSTINATO

HAMP

Lionel Hampton, circa 1945,
wearing a ham and eggs
sunset on his tie. From his teeth
flash beautiful visions
of Buddha walking on milk bottles!

MJQ

She walks along the garden path
between the battlements of roses,
hands clasped, a frown
upon her brow. The breeze
of that lost summer trails her
silks behind her, her satin shoes
dampen on the morning grass.
She hears, beyond the wall,
the clank of knights at jousting.

She stops - her frown not
now of worry, but of puzzlement.
And all around her swirls the sunlight
amongst the jitterbugging leaves.

JACKIE McLEAN

The scene's McLean!
McLean is the scene!

With his taut passion,
he blows his
long driving lines
and takes us on a journey
we hope will never end.

Will life escape
the acid rain
that burns the forests,
sours the lakes?

In his small hemisphere
he sucks the poison
from the air.

Come on, you cats,
tune-in out there!
Forget the schmeck
that's messing up
your minds!
Beat your weapons
into saxophones!

He holds us
'til the wee hours.
And then he smiles
and places his sax-case
on the back seat of a cab.
And folds into the night.

It's all right, Officer,
we're clean!
The scene's McLean,
McLean's the scene!

FINALE

Now they're starting up
Jumping with Symphony Sid
and they're going to keep it going
for three whole days!
Bassists and baritone
saxophonists
lugging their instruments
through the streets,
queuing at the door
to have a blow ...

But *we* can't stay that long.
The music fades away
into our dreams.
Fades away
into our dreams.

ADDITIONAL POEMS

BIRD LIVES

Chas Foote. Somewhere off Shaftesbury Avenue.
Circa 1953. Everyone is buying altos.
Some will play them. Some will be
quite good. Some will keep them
under the bed for a year or two then sell them.

After they found
that getting a sound
was not too easy.

Everyone was buying altos. The guy
was showing them how to work the keys.
Outside, the plane trees shivered gently
in the sad September sunshine.

FOR BILLIE HOLIDAY

"Don't worry 'bout me." This is
the eternal sadness. How she
leans on the words she sings.
She, newly risen from the Earth.
Unique in her being;
about to fall back
into the endless flow
and being given no second chance
to be the same.
Something else would rise, yes.
A tree. A bird, in aeons to come.
But not her again, ever.
Not her. Sighing and staggering
on the words.

Published in OSTINATO

MY MELLOPHONE

My mellophone is round and smooth,
coiled like a sea-snail.
At rest, the sounds of the sea
sough through its mysterious length,
lingering in its secret caverns.

When I blow, growths of sound
stir and thrust like alien weeds
against the sun. Soon a whole
exotic forest fills the room
and jewelled birds answer my call.

A key-change brings life's sadnesses
before my eyes. Goodbyes
and deaths, the loss of love.
But greenery coils around me,
whose sap absolves my pain.

At the end of the afternoon
music lies scattered on the floor.
Silence falls like a shroud.
Beneath my fingers, the valves
clank like old armour.

Published in OSTINATO

THIN POEM FOR WARDELL GRAY - 1

Wardell wailed
his long lines ...
lines like roots,
twisting and
turning thru
history,

or like lines
of light that
curve around
the cosmos
but never
form a circle.

Wardell wailed
and maybe
his lines were
just like the
journey of
a train, that

one day ran
out of steam
and stopped in
a patch of
beautiful
countryside.

The spirits
of countless
other great
engines are
waiting in
the sidings.

Published in OSTINATO

THIN POEM FOR WARDELL GRAY - 2

I imagine luxuries
that last for ever
when I hear your
long loping lines –
beautiful journeys
through spacious
landscapes; villages
where kids play
hopscotch
on sunlit afternoons.

Sometimes.
benevolent serpents
of the imagination
twine through
labyrinths of foliage.
Jack's bean-stalk
grows and grows;
old, weed grown
railway tracks
wind endlessly
to nowhere,
carrying ghosts
of long-dead trains.

But it's more than that
(or less than that).
Words scratch the
surface only
or destroy the thing
they try to understand.

Leave it to you,
Wardell;
your rhythms and
the routes you took
through chord progressions.

Your smiling face
on old record-sleeves.

Published in OSTINATO

BAM!

I haven't heard any bebop
for three days ...
OK, the hillside
stands against the sky,
birds twitter in zig-zag perspectives
through the afternoon;
a distant stream
rustles like silk
in the slow golden stillness;
there is peace here
like I never knew before -
but I haven't heard any bebop
for three days ...

Bud Powell, Charlie Parker,
Fats Navarro, Don Lamphere -
they all come crowding
in the room.
Hey man, they say, come on,
you haven't heard any bebop
for three days ...

Published in SINGING BRINK (by Arvon)

FOR CHARLIE PARKER

You could say that trash-cans
consistently spawn forth life ...
You could say that we all came
from some gigantic trash-heap.
Life must have dirt. You don't get
amoeba in distilled water ...
The whole city looks like trash:
vacant lots strewn with broken
bricks, dirty grey tenements;
dead leaves and cigarette ends
littering the sidewalks, black
greasy water in the gutters ...
And, Bird, your music burst forth
from a trash-heap called a city;
rose up and sped towards
the rising sun ...

LITTLE QUASIMODO

I

I standin' by me father's grave,
sax case on thee groun' beside me.
On a crooked tree flowers smile
an' little birds sing songs from Heaven.

Me father was straight and tall;
no Rasta mock him, no skinhead
chase *him* through the streets. He
growin' crooked now but still in sunshine.

Hey, Li'l Quasimodo! Rasta call,
Where you goin' wid you saxophone?
But on lamp-lit nights me hunchback
throw huge an' frightenin' shadow.

Me mother work big hotel kitchen;
she and other women singin' while
they work. She hands movin' slower
on account of she arthritis.

We live in two rooms
top of thee hotel. I practise there
on me battered saxophone,
sometimes songs me mother sings.

Thee porter rappin' on thee door.
*Hey, Hootie, manager say
you quit you hollerin' now -
people comin' in for dinner.*

II

On me way to music lesson,
Rasta call me from they club.
Hey, Li'l Quasimodo, they call.
Where you goin' wid you saxophone?

I walk on, but they call me more.
Li'l Quasimodo, Li'l Quasimodo,
come an' hab a blow wid us.
Let's hear what you got to say!

III

Me bebop. They reggae. Strange shiftin'
rhythm. Me gaunt shadow mingle
with thee flickering shadows
of thee dancing Rastafari ...

I hear me music like a bird,
flyin' above me father's grave. I hear
me mother's songs. An' no one
worry 'bout me crooked back.

ME YONGA BRUDDA

Me yonga brudda highly unconventional;
he shorn he dreadlock, man;
he wearin' mean black beret
an' always sportin' shades.
He eschew da funky reggae rhythm.

It's true he smoke da ganja,
but I and I never see him
hangin' roun' da neighbourhood
like he used to all natty dread,
smilin' at da funky reggae rhythm.

Nah, me brudda very different now.
He playin' da tenor saxophone,
runnin' up an' down da scales all day,
an' we muvva confused by it all -
he jazz, me funky reggae rhythm.

He speak these names me never heard.
Eric Dolphy, man, an' John Coltrane.
He know some pretty sharp fellows,
but every one of dem so unusual -
nah dreadlock, nah funky reggae rhythm.

But nah ofay will rip me brudda off.
He playin' so fast an' furious
none of dem could ever follow him.
I and I proud of me brudda really,
in spite of he lack funky reggae rhythm.

THE BIG FOOT SONG

When you hear the crashing of branches
In the forest -
That's Big Foot.

When you hear a-grunting and a-snuffling
In the darkness -
That's Big Foot.

When you see the shifting of the sunlight
In the shadows -
That's Big Foot.

When you get a funny kind of feeling
You're being watched -
That's Big Foot.

> But you're never going to see him,
> Though you'll hear him lumbering by.
> You're never going to see him -
> Because he's far too shy.

When you hear a haunting kind of cry
Up on the mountain -
That's Big Foot.

But, don't worry, he ain't gonna hurt you -
He's a nice guy -
He's Big Foot.

Published in YELLOW CRANE

THIS IS THE LIFE
(Tubby Hayes as a Country Station Master)

A bird sings bebop on the station roof,
a farm-truck trundles down the lane.
Tubby reaches for his waistcoat pocket,
hauls his watch out on its golden chain.

He gazes fondly over corn-fields,
with half-a-chuckle, half-a-sigh,
to where a distant flock of rooks
makes lazy patterns in the sky.

The first train of the day is due;
he clips tickets at the wicket gate;
soon blows his whistle, waves his flag,
and doesn't worry if the train is late.

He saunters up and down the platform;
soon time for lunch and then the 3:15.
In a corner of the station master's office
his saxophone, half-forgotten, leans.

(Apparently, at one time Tubby Hayes
thought he'd pack it all in and become
a country station-master where not
many trains stopped and he'd just have
to clip a few tickets.)

Published in OTHER POETRY

DAWN

The saxophone player
on the rusted fire-escape
blows blues into the dawn.

The mountains are too far
for any echo,
except in imagination.

A newsboy in the street below
drops yesterday
through peoples' doors.

An early-morning drunk
upsets a bin; the lid
clatters down the sidewalk.

Against this outrage,
the dawn, for an instant,
holds back the day.

WHEN I HEAR ORNEITE COLEMAN'S 'THE BLESSING'

When I hear Ornette Coleman's 'The Blessing'
I feel I am back
in the streets of the old city,
saying my last goodbyes
to Ahmed and Ali and Sulieman
and Aboud the Wise.

We remembered the time we took sherbet
in a date-palm's purple shadow,
while sleek gyrating odalisques
danced for our tired eyes;
for Ahmed and Ali and Sulieman
and Aboud the Wise.

We spoke of how once, when the sunset
lay like a jewel on the desert,
I promised I'd be like a brother for ever,
even when far under distant skies,
to Ahmed and Ali and Sulieman
and Aboud the Wise.

But now they're long gone, those times,
and I live in a land far away.
Almost forgotten now the sea of sand
where the secret oasis lies -
and Ahmed and Ali and Sulieman
and Aboud the Wise.

JOE HARRIOT

He knew the tunes all right
but wanted to go his own way;
wanted to make something new
the world would remember.

Shake Keane tapped his wineglass
and Joe picked up on it;
started a whole new thing,
a universe of sound.

Now that music of tomorrow
is half-a-century old
and as mellow as birdsong
and summer fields.

It still speaks of memories
and laughter; vision
of palm leaves and oleander,
impossible white walls.

Yet sometimes light splinters
as his alto screams. Aura
of pain and rejection
and a path of no end.

It seems there's nothing new
in this world - only freedom.
The birds know all about it
and still sing his song.

MILES

Layers of association
cover the original meaning of music,
which had no meaning
yet meant everything.

All Blues. A gramophone on a spindly-legged table
on a loose floorboard;
the needle jerked
when someone crossed the room.

Sea shells on a salty sill,
yachts out on a blue bay.
The LP sleeve sellotaped together,
scuffed round the edges.

The sound of his horn like sunlight
slicing through shadow, like something else,
like words never spoken;
like *Oh God, got to have more of this!*

Yet I'm not sure when or where
I first heard that tune; who with
and what promises were made
in a summer that was never going to end.

Perhaps from someone's *Dansette* record player
at a party in a barn in 1960
where we smoked a bit of weed
and messed about in the straw.

Could've been anywhere.
Maybe that cafe where we met each week
on Fridays after work.
Or just twiddling the dial on a late night radio.

Or maybe the first time
I heard *All Blues*
was in a record shop in Charing Cross Road,
stripped of everything but itself.

THE CREATOR

You never meant it to be like this.
Or maybe you did.
We've written books about it,
which fill shelves in dusty libraries.

Light breezes would tremble tree tops,
rain would be sweet and occasional.
Lions would eat fruit; *homo sapiens*
would hug each other; play music
in praise of something they hadn't fathomed.

Ah well, shadows lengthen on the grass,
bird song heralds a long slow evening.
In the morning newspapers will be empty of news;
well - there'd be GOOD NEWS.

I don't suppose you meant it like that at all.
Maybe Charlie Parker knew this
and that was his undoing.

BODY LANGUAGE
for Pete White

Square white buildings, picked out in light and
shadow, seem arranged like a cubist composition
against a long low line of purple hills.
Solar panels dazzle and a solitary wind turbine
turns half-heartedly. As I prepare my striped
towel and a glass of cold beer, someone
comes out on to a rooftop on the other side
of town; sunlight glints on something he is
holding - a saxophone, alto or tenor I can't
see which at this distance; and his music is
lost amidst the intervening sounds of the
afternoon: the murmur of traffic, someone
laughing in an apartment across the street,
the rustling of leaves and the slow whispering
of the wind. But I can guess from the way
he leans back, and, from the movement of his
tiny puppet arms, that it must be bebop.

POT CROIDLE
for Pete Burden

The saxophone player
on a rusted fire escape
plays blues into the morning,

across city rooftops
and out into the world beyond,
ringed by distant mountains.

Alleyways still hold shadows
but golden sunlight
strikes walls of whitewashed houses.

A newsboy in the street below
drops yesterday
through peoples' doors.

Curtains are drawn back
and doors slam; a naked figure
moves behind a window.

A dustbin lid clatters
somewhere down a street;
someone drops a scaffolding pole.

A radio comes on
with news that no one hears
beyond the hissing of a kettle.

A bird sings in a tree,
answered by another on an TV aerial;
a cat stalks along a fence.

Now a car starts up
and someone shouts;
a cyclist rings his bell.

Laughing children
run around a corner;
a dog barks far away.

A figure moves across
a distant rooftop garden;
in back yards neighbours natter.

The sax man plays a final chorus;
we can almost hear
an echo from the mountains.

PETE LIVES!

ABOUT THE AUTHOR

John Wyndham Tatum, born in Edinburgh in 1933 managed to snatch bits of Louis Armstrong, Tommy Dorsey and Artie Shaw off the radio in a household where jazz was frowned upon. He took up the trumpet while on service in the RAF in Cyprus in the 1950s.

He played and sat in with bands in various pubs in Brighton after demob, which is how he met the altoist Pete Burden, whose quartet played on the BBC broadcast of 'Poems to Sundry Notes of Jazz'. His hobby is painting watercolours.

Now, at the age of 86, he is in a care home in Brighton, living in a room high above the rooftops listening to Charlie Parker. He now plays the conga drum in place of the trumpet in weekly jam sessions at the home and is writing a book about the RAF, entitled 'Your Turn to Make the Tea, Sarge'

"Jazz life proper started in the early 50s when I went to Studio 51 in London and heard the Jimmy Skidmore Sextet with Dill Jones and Terry Brown. Skid was always my favourite British musician because, to my ears, he sounded like Wardell Gray. I also went to the White Lion in Edgeware on Sundays to hear the exciting Toni Anton Kenton-style big band. Five years followed in the RAF where there was a lot of jazz going on—and I could write a book about it.

I bought my first trumpet with my first week's pay from the RAF and took it to Cyprus with me. I couldn't really play in those days, but after demob I took a few lessons from a trumpet teacher just off Piccadilly Circus. Coincidentally, he also taught trumpet at Radley, a public school when my brother was the physics master. I also went regularly to the newly-opened Ronnie Scott's club where I saw and heard everybody.

I first got to know Pete Burden, whose quartet played on my jazz and poetry gig, when, back in the 60s, I cheekily asked to sit in with the band, led by the Hastings pianist Pete White, at a concert at Brighton Art College. After that I used to go to Hastings to sit in with the 'two Petes' at various venues in and around the town. Pete White is a brilliantly creative pianist with a very profound knowledge of harmony.

Pete Burden and I, and a few others, used to go to all-nighters at Ronnie Scott's in London where we heard and saw such American greats as Zoot Sims, Dexter Gordon, Rahsaan Roland Kirk and Sonny Rollins. Sonny Rollins once came into the club blowing his saxophone all the way downstairs from the street outside. In the first pale light of dawn us Sussex lads had breakfast in an all-night café just off Trafalgar Square.

Some years later, I found myself playing with a jazz/rock group named 'Garudas' - after an Indonesian Eagle God. We played at the Black Rock 'Bathing Machine' on Sundays and at other venues around Brighton. Before that I had taken part in the regular Sunday afternoon jam sessions at the Norfolk Arms, where I first met most of the people I now know. And sometimes the late great Vic Richards would let me sit in for the odd number at his regular spot at the King and Queen!

I was a member of the Brighton Jazz Cooperative for several years and had the privilege of being taught by such luminaries as Adrian Kendon, Geoff Simpkins, Harry Beckett, Ian Hamer and Trevor Kaye. I very much enjoyed this experience, although I could never really get my head round the chord sequences!

The great American saxist and flautist, Lawrence Jones, sometimes let me sit in on his band at the Sussex Arts Club and various other venues, and I once played a whole session with Herbie Flower's band at the Sussex Arts Club. The drummer Tony Riordan got me that gig."

Printed in Poland
by Amazon Fulfillment
Poland Sp. z o.o., Wrocław

60095320R00035